Little Duck's Moving Day

by Stephanie Calmenson
illustrated by Kathy Cruickshank

A GOLDEN BOOK • NEW YORK

Western Publishing Company, Inc., Racine, Wisconsin 53404

When Little Duck woke up each morning, the first thing he looked at was the picture of three gray mice on his wall. This morning, Little Duck whispered to them, "Today is a special day."

"Good morning, Little Duck," said his mother. "Are you ready for moving day?"

Little Duck nodded.

"I've made your favorite breakfast," said Mrs. Duck. "Now, let's dress quickly. We have a lot to do before the movers come."

While they were eating, there was a knock at the door. It was Rabbit and his mother.

"Hello, Rabbit," said Little Duck. "I'm moving today."

"I know," said Rabbit. "I came to say good-bye and ask if I could visit at your new house."

Little Duck looked at his mother.
"Of course you can visit," said Mrs.
Duck. "We hope you'll come very soon."

After breakfast, it was time to pack. Little Duck started to fill a box with his toys.

"Good-bye, green spaceman," he said.

"How about saying, 'See you later?'"
suggested Mrs. Duck. Little Duck liked that
better.

"See you later, toys," he said when the
box was full.

Beep! Beep! went a horn outside. The movers had come.

"Look at that big truck!" said Little Duck. Then he asked, "Mommy, will they take away my bed?"

"Yes. It will go into your new room," said Mrs. Duck.

"Will they take away my lamp?" asked
Little Duck.

"Yes. It will go into your new room,
too."

"Will they take away my picture?" asked
Little Duck.

"Yes. It…"

Mrs. Duck did not finish what she was saying because Little Duck had started to cry.

"I don't want them to take away my picture!" he said.

"Then you can carry it," said his mother. "And we'll put it on your wall at the new house."

The movers started their work. They went in and out of the house, carrying boxes. Soon the rooms were empty, except for one thing—Little Duck's picture.

Mrs. Duck took the picture down and gave it to Little Duck.

Little Duck waved good-bye to his house.

He kept on waving even when he couldn't see the house any more. Then he fell asleep.

When Little Duck opened his eyes again he saw his new house.

Again the movers went in and out, in and out, carrying boxes. Soon the new house was full.

"Now, Mommy?" said Little Duck.
"Yes, now we can hang your picture,"
said Little Duck's mommy.

By the time Little Duck was ready to go
to bed, his new room looked just right.

"I think you'll be happy here," said
Little Duck's mother.

Little Duck thought so, too.